June 2010

Ian.
Thank-you for coming to my 2nd Birthday party! Alexander

Billy Bully

A school-yard counting tale.

To all the people I love. — A.G.

For my son, Oliver — S.S.

Library of Congress Cataloging-in-Publication Data available.

ISBN-13: 978-0-545-11012-9
ISBN-10: 0-545-11012-2

10 9 8 7 6 5 4 3 2 1 09 10 11 12 13

Printed in the U.S.A. 23
First printing, July 2009

Billy Bully

A school-yard counting tale.

By Alvaro & Ana Galan
Illustrated by Steve Simpson

SCHOLASTIC INC.
New York Toronto London Auckland Sydney
Mexico City New Delhi Hong Kong Buenos Aires

When Billy Bully comes to play,

School

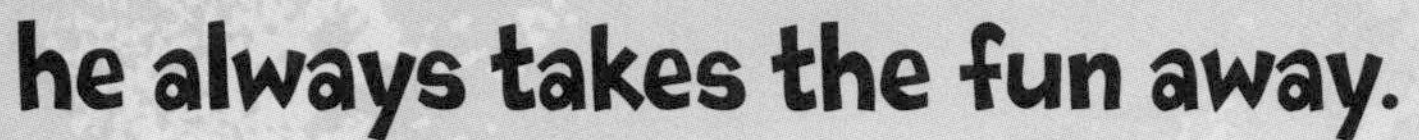

he always takes the fun away.

He grabs a toy and says, “It’s mine!”
And so his friends are down to 9.

He cuts the line and thinks he's great.
And so his friends are down to 8.

He pouts, and screams, and pushes Evan.
And so his friends are down to 7.

He takes and breaks their pick-up sticks.
And so his friends are down to 6.

He picks up speed and takes a dive.
And so his friends are down to 5.

He hogs the ball and shoots to score.
And so his friends are down to 4.

He locks the door and hides the key.
And so his friends are down to 3.

He scares the frog when he says, "Boo!"
And so his friends are down to 2.

He won't take turns and says he's won.
And so his friends are down to 1.

He squashes Chick (he weighs a ton).
And so his friends are down to none!

Billy Bully wants to play
but everyone has run away.

Now Billy Bully's feeling blue.
Until –
he figures out just what to do.

He says to Sheep, “It’s you who won.”
And now his friends are up to 1!

He says to Rabbit, "This is for you."
And now his friends are up to 2!

He says to Horse, "Please play with me."
And now his friends are up to 3!

He shares his food when Pig wants more.
And now his friends are up to 4!

He gently teaches Duck to dive.
And now his friends are up to 5!

He makes Chick laugh and shows her tricks.
And now his friends are up to 6!

He gets the ball, passes to Evan,
and now his friends are up to 7!

He waits for Dog and holds the gate.
And now his friends are up to 8!

He doesn't push and waits in line.
And now his friends are up to 9!

He says to Frog, "Let's try again."
And now his friends are up to 10!

When Billy **Bull** learns how to play,
all his friends come back to stay.

Dear Parents and Teachers,

Most children encounter bullying every single day. Contrary to conventional wisdom, both bullies and victims of bullying suffer. For bullies, their behavior often reveals underlying problems, such as low self-esteem or anxiety. They may also be overwhelmed with family or school problems and have a hard time controlling their emotions. When bullies are unable to express their worries or concerns directly, they may cope by hurting others. Likewise, victims of bullying may feel scared, helpless, ashamed, or sad. These children may not know how to assert themselves, how to avoid being bullied, or how to seek help by telling an adult.

As parents and teachers, it is our responsibility to learn to identify and stop bullying behavior whenever possible. It is often necessary to confront the bully directly, contact parents, and involve school officials. Besides setting limits and consequences for children who bully others, all children involved need to be given emotional support. Bullies should be encouraged to talk to a trusted adult about their worries or concerns. Victims should be taught the skills to help them cope with future bullying and be encouraged to talk about their feelings, too. Children who are bullies or victims of bullying can express their feelings through play, storytelling games, or drawing.

Parents and teachers can become role models by managing their reactions and responses to others, and by refusing to tolerate harmful teasing in the classroom or at home. They can model respect and openness by creating an environment where it's okay to share feelings. By consciously addressing the causes and effects of bullying, we will provide our children with exactly what they deserve: a safe space to learn and grow.

— Ellen Jacobs, Ph.D., Clinical Social Work